God Gave Us Easter

by Lisa Tawn Bergren   art by Laura J. Bryant

WATERBROOK
PRESS

GOD GAVE US EASTER

Scripture quotations or paraphrases are taken from the Holy Bible, New International Version®, NIV®. Copyright © 1973, 1978, 1984 by Biblica Inc.™ Used by permission of Zondervan. All rights reserved worldwide. www.zondervan.com.

Hardcover ISBN 978-0-307-73072-5
eBook ISBN 978-0-307-73111-1

Text copyright © 2012 by Lisa Tawn Bergren

Illustrations copyright © 2012 by Laura Bryant

Cover design by Mark D. Ford; cover illustration by Laura J. Bryant

Published in the United States by WaterBrook, an imprint of the Crown Publishing Group, a division of Penguin Random House LLC, New York.

WATERBROOK® and its deer colophon are registered trademarks of Penguin Random House LLC.

Library of Congress Cataloging-in-Publication Data
Bergren, Lisa Tawn.
    God gave us Easter / by Lisa Tawn Bergren ; illustrated by Laura Bryant.
        p. cm.
    Summary: Polar bear Little Cub talks with her father and learns about God's design for the Easter season and what it really means to Little Cub and her family.
    ISBN 978-0-307-73072-5 — ISBN 978-0-307-73111-1 (electronic)
    [1. Easter—Fiction. 2. Christian life—Fiction. 3. Polar bear—Fiction. 4. Bears—Fiction.] I. Bryant, Laura J., ill. II. Title.
    PZ7.B452233God 2013
    [E]—dc23
                                                    2012020069

Printed in the United States of America
2017

For Ava and Wrenna.

May you know the full promise of Easter!

~Aunt Lisa

"I love Easter," Little Cub said.

"Me too," Papa Bear said. "It's even better than Christmas."

"Better than *Christmas*? Why?"

"Because on Christmas, we celebrate Jesus' birthday. But on Easter, we remember we get to be with him forever."

"Forever?"

"Forever. That's why God gave us Easter."

"I like the Easter Bunny!" cried Little Cub's little sister.

"And candy!" added Little Cub's little brother.

"The Easter Bunny is like Santa," Papa Bear said. "He reminds us of gifts and happy surprises in the morning. But God is the one who gave us Easter. Easter is part of a bigger story he had in mind for a long, long time."

"How did God give us Easter, Papa?"

"See this egg?" Papa Bear said. "It's a symbol. Helping us remember. Just like the shell cracks open and a chick comes out, we remember that Jesus was in a tomb…but he didn't stay dead."

"He didn't?"

"No. Even death couldn't trap God's Son.
He is life itself. And God loved us so much,
he wanted us to be with him always. We can
see signs of his Easter plan all around us."

Little Cub and Papa went on a hike. They found a big tree that had fallen over in a storm.

"God told his people that Jesus would come from one family. 'The Root of Jesse,' he was called. Jesse and his wife had children, and they had children, and *they* had children."

"And one of them was Jesus?"

"Yes, Little Cub. All along, God knew he would give us Easter."

"It's sad this big ol' tree fell down and died," Little Cub said.

"Yes," Papa said. "But when it did, it made room for new little trees to grow. See how the sun shines now, without those big branches to block it?"

"And how all the pine cones fell across the forest floor? These pine cones will spread their seeds, and baby trees will grow like this one. Out of death, comes life. That's how God wants us to see Easter."

"I still don't like dying."

"Neither do I. We were born to love life. God loves life. But sometimes we have to let go of one thing so we can move on to another."

"For instance, think about this river. Where do rivers go, Little Cub?"

"To the ocean!" Little Cub loved the ocean.

"Yes! The river ends, but it spreads into something even bigger. Heaven is like the ocean for us. Because God gave us Easter, we can be a part of Something Bigger—and even though we talk to Jesus now, in heaven we will *see* Jesus face to face."

"Couldn't Jesus have just waited for us in heaven?"

"A long time ago, God's children wouldn't listen to him. They didn't even believe in him anymore. It made God very sad and angry. So he sent a huge flood to start anew with Noah and his family."

"In that ark with polar bears?"

"And giraffes and monkeys and turtles!"

"And when the flood was done, God promised never to send another one."

"Whew," Little Cub said with relief. "That's good." Little Cub liked water, but she liked land too.

"It *is* good. After the flood, God gave us a rainbow as a sign of his promise. But when his children, who said they'd follow him, were disobedient again, he had to find a way to keep us connected, once and for all. God wants nothing more than to be close to us, his children."

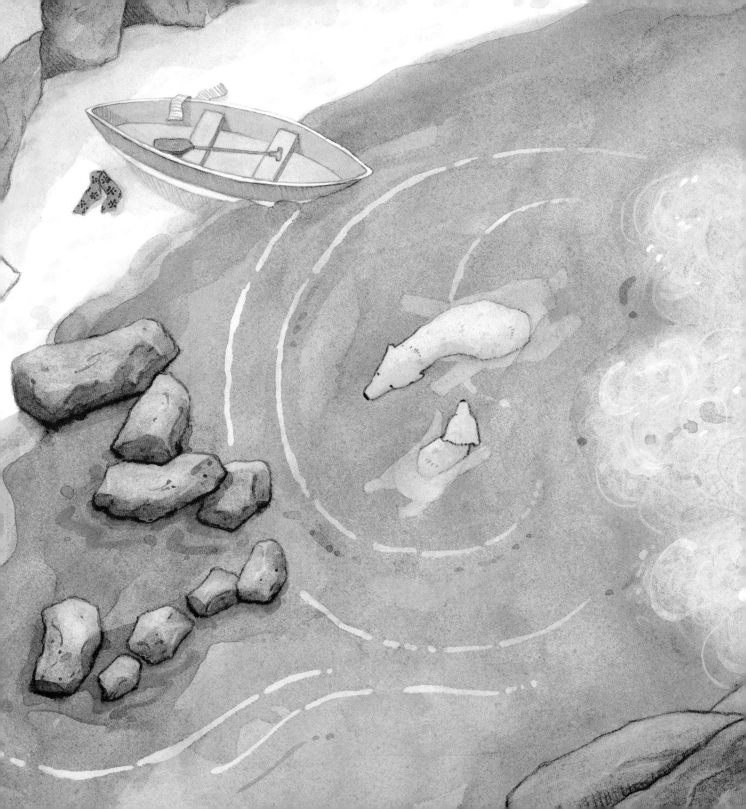

"So Jesus keeps the promise we broke, Little Cub. And because of him, God forgives us when we make bad choices."

"All of us?"

"Everyone who believes in him. That's how God gave us Easter."

"Do you talk to Jesus, Papa?"

"Every day," Papa Bear said. "All day."

"Does he talk back?"

"In a way. It's like he whispers in my heart."

"In your heart? I thought we listened with our *ears*."

"We do, but to hear Jesus, it takes a special kind of listening."

Little Cub was silent for the rest of the walk home.
She was trying to listen with her heart.

She listened…

And listened…

And listened.

That night, as Papa and Mama tucked her into bed, she was still listening. And as her parents kissed her and hugged her, she turned over and remembered she was God's child too.

In that moment, she felt comfy and cozy and cared for, almost as if Jesus had whispered *I love you* in her heart.

"I love you too, Jesus," Little Cub whispered. "Thanks for giving us Easter."

The next morning, Little Cub
said, "Papa, I think I heard
God last night."

"You did?" he said, putting his arm
around her. "Well that's the best
Easter present ever! What'd he say?"

"I love you."

"Mmm, those are good words.
Perfect words. And they really
are what Easter is all about."

Enjoy the rest of the God Gave Us series!

Available in eBook:

Available in Print:

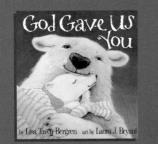

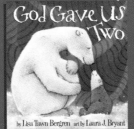

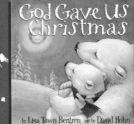

3-in-1 Treasury!

Available as Board Book: